This book belongs to:

_____

Hello Baseball

WRITTEN BY
DESTINY PHILLIP

ILLUSTRATED BY
WHIMSICAL DESIGNS BY CJ

In loving memory of our Papa, Milford Lee Hayes, Sr.
We love and miss you dearly.

All rights reserved. Published in the United States by Francis & Lee Publishing, La Plata, MD.

Library of Congress Cataloging-in-Publication Data

Destiny Phillip, author

Whimsical Designs by CJ, illustrator

Library of Congress Control Number: 2021912660

ISBN 978-1-7371124-0-2 (hardcover), ISBN 978-1-7371124-1-9 (ebook)

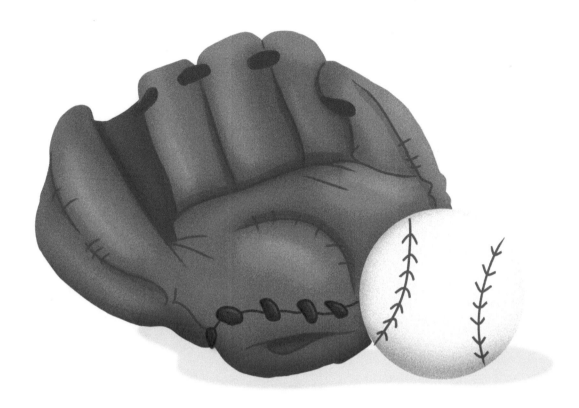

This story is about a grandfather enjoying a day with his grandkids.

Papa's great-grandsons are spending the summer at Gram and Papa's house.

"Hey Sport, let's do something fun together," says Papa.

Looking slightly interested, but still focused on the video game, Raiden says, "Papa I don't want to stop playing video games."

Papa does not understand why the boys are so captivated...

Papa explains, "Yes, I know video games are cool,
but I know something much cooler. Follow me..."

On their way, they bump into Jayce. Papa tells him to stop running around the house. "Running is for outside," says Papa.

Jayce, out of breath from running, pauses and responds,
"But Papa, I need my exercise and running is super cool."

Papa explains, "Well, I know something much cooler. Follow us..."

Bash and Drew are playing on the porch. Papa says,
"Boys, playing with trucks is cool, but I know something much cooler."

Bash and Drew join their cousins and follow Papa.

To Papa's surprise, the twins are sitting down quietly watching their favorite cartoon. They are not too happy about turning off the T.V.

Papa says, "I know – I know, cartoons are really cool, but I know something much cooler."

Finally, Papa has all eight of his great-grandsons together and ready to explore "something much cooler."

Their adventure begins.

Papa drives to City Mills Park. The boys are so excited.

Papa says, "Okay boys, let's play some good old-fashioned baseball. Baseball is muuuuuch cooler than video games and television."

But Papa, "I don't think I can hit the ball," explains Bash.

"Yes, you can Bash, be patient son,"
Papa says, showing him how to swing the bat.

Drew chimes in,
"My mommy said I can do all things through Christ. Let me try."

"...that's exactly right grasshopper, you guys can do all things through Christ, and always remember that," explains Papa.

The boys have a great time running the bases, batting and catching the ball in the field. It starts getting dark. It is time to return home for dinner.

They arrive home, where Gram just finished grilling food.

Grandma says, "Boys, go wash your hands and get ready to eat."

After saying grace, everyone begins eating the yummy food.

They chat about their fantastic day playing baseball and how Papa made it cool.

CPSIA information can be obtained
at www.ICGtesting.com
Printed in the USA
LVHW021935071021
699747LV00001B/6